For Katherine and Ant

First published 2008 by Walker Books Ltd
87 Vauxhall Walk, London SE11 5HJ

2 4 6 8 10 9 7 5 3 1

This book has been typeset in Gill Sans MT Schoolbook.

Printed in China.

British Library Cataloguing in Publication Data:
a catalogue record for this book is available
from the British Library.

ISBN 978-1-4063-0907-2

www.walkerbooks.co.uk

Tilly and
her friends
all live
together in
a little yellow
house...

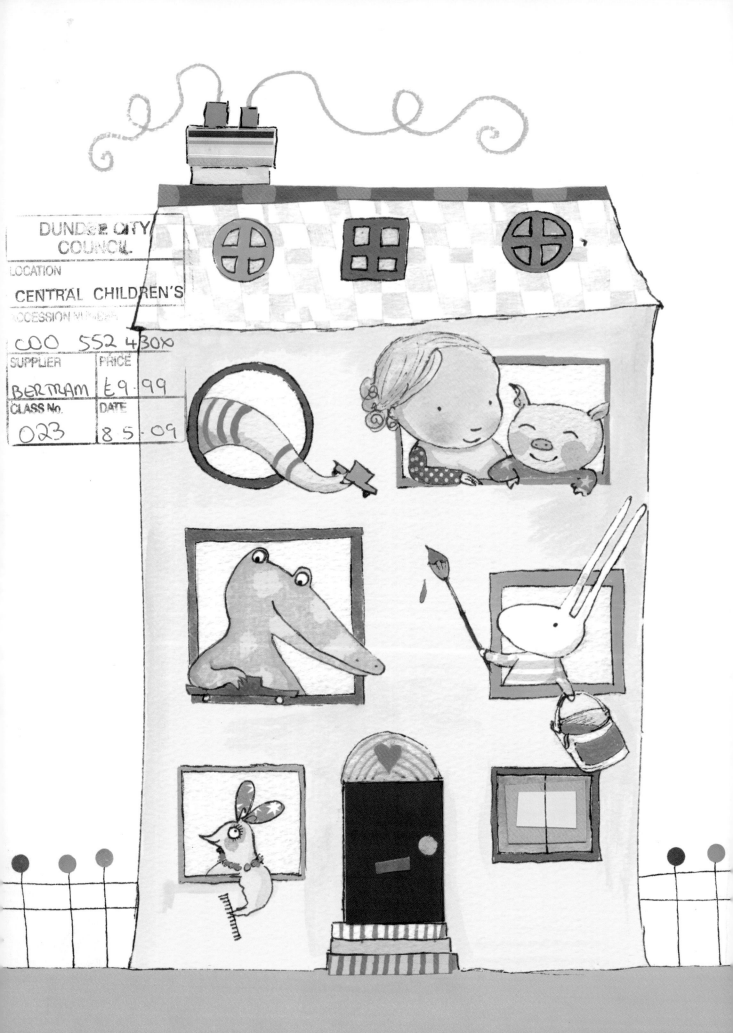

Happy
Hector

Polly Dunbar

WALKER BOOKS
AND SUBSIDIARIES
LONDON • BOSTON • SYDNEY • AUCKLAND

Hector
was sitting on
Tilly's lap.

"I am the

happiest

I have ever

been!"

he said.

Tumpty and Doodle were happy too.

They were playing cars.

Pru was happily combing her feathers.

And Tiptoe was happy painting a
wonderful picture.

"Come and paint
with **me!**"
he said.

"No thanks," said Hector.

"We're **happy** sitting here."

But Tiptoe **really**
wanted to play with Tilly.

So he hopped on to Tilly's lap.

"Oh," said Hector.

"Look at them having fun,"
said Doodle.

"Let's join in!"

"**Oh no,**" said Hector.

Hector went off to be alone.

"Now I am the unhappiest I have ever been," he said.

"Will you play cars with me?"

asked Doodle.

"Can I comb your ears?"

asked Pru.

"Can I paint your nose blue?"
asked Tiptoe.

"NO YOU CAN'T!"
said Hector.

"Can I sit on your lap?"
asked Tumpty.

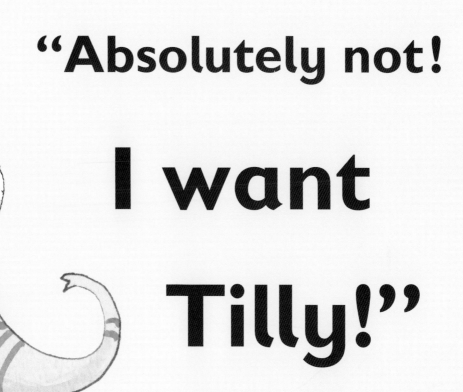

"Absolutely not!

I want

Tilly!"

cried Hector.

But Tilly was busy ...

painting a wonderful picture ...

... of Hector!

"Wow!" said Hector.

Hector was happy.

So happy,

he even let Tiptoe

paint his nose

blue.

Then Hector sat
on Tilly's lap.

"Now," he said,

"I am the

happiest

happiest

I have ever

been!"

The End